Eradicated.

Tilda Almqvist

Zero, here is the context

He does not just hate the monarchy

INTRODUCTION

Teivel Malacoda had acted as an advisor, and friend, to King Harald for a long time, having found a beginning to their friendship at the respective ages of twelve and fourteen. It had all begun when Teivel's father sought out a job as a royal guard, while his mother picked up work as a servant, jobs they soon left behind, but the two boys were quick friends. Not long after, they both died after a nasty altercation with a vendor at the yearly market, *after hours*. They had heard of something called the midnight market after the day's wares had run dry, they had not been expecting wares with magical abilities to be sold by those *with* magical abilities. Once their true colors reached the surface, it did not take long for things to take a bloody turn. Teivel found them the next day, bodies dragged beneath a tree. Fifteen years old. He ran up to the castle after that, asking for any guard who would look his way to help him, tell him what to do. And Harald, as any thirteen year old boy who found his closest friend in such a state would do, offered to let him stay in the castle, promising to keep him by his side for as long as they both lived. And he did.

But what about before? It was clear some form of hatred or distaste existed within Teivel's parents, and surely Teivel himself. That takes us back to Gloh, where he had been born and raised for the first fourteen years of his life. His parents almost the entirety of theirs, sans one.

Gloh, a small region consisting of a singular village in a small valley dividing the land ahead from the mountains above. Small as it was, they had raked up quite the reputation due to their absolute hatred of all types of magic. Color magic, Delvi magic, demons. Anything and everything they deemed '*unnatural*', was in their eyes something that must be eradicated no matter the cost.

Nobody knows why this opinion was formed, but they are all aware of the effect it had on the outside world. Centuries ago, they were rather loud with that opinion, making sure everyone knew by hunting down and killing any and all magic users they could find. They started in Kleurstark with little objection from the people who were unaffected, but when they tried to expand… Oh, that did not go well. Kleurstark is easy to conquer in comparison to the other two continents of Delviann, and Enield, where magic existed freely. And predominantly.

They were quick to fight back, an easy feat against such a small group of people, even with the blood of hundreds on their hands. The battle was lost before it had even truly begun, sending the small region back into its valley, where it has since remained without another outburst of hatred. The havoc they had caused would soon be forgotten by most, lingering near the back of their heads but less so as the generations passed. But if magic ran through your veins, you knew, and you were wary of the villagers from the mountain valley. It didn't matter how kind and well-meaning someone appeared to be, hatred like that was more than taught, it was engrained, practically genetic.

AGE: 46

The yearly market came, well, every year. It was as big of an event each time, especially considering how the royal family had created tradition in attending. Rows of stalls filled to the brim with different wares and oddities, villagers from all over the continent flooded the central village where the market took place. It was a market without a name, but trust, it will soon be given one.

As per usual, the royal family has headed down to the grand market an hour after sunrise. King Harald, his wife, Queen Dolores, and their ten-year-old boy, Prince Anwir. Future king of Gortasia. King Harald's loyal advisor, however, remained behind in the castle, as he always did, year after year. Not once had he ventured to the market, never less the village. The images of his parents haunted him, the sounds of his own screams upon finding their wrangled, bloodied bodies, the wetness of the tears on his face. The ultimate hatred that sprouted inside of him, beginning to grow, continuing to this day, and until the day of his demise. But that's not just yet. No.

Although he held nothing but respect and well wishes for the man who had saved him from a life on the street, given him a lifelong job, and home, the same did not go for his wife. He had not found Dolores to be anything other than kind, loving, and a wonderful match to Harald when they had first met. It wasn't until years later, after they had gotten married, after they had had their first child together. Two years ago, was the moment his suspicion began to form, a subtle hatred deep down inside of him which would slowly bubble up to the surface until it consumed him. He had seen something inside of her that night, something evil. Only that could have killed their unborn child and rid her body of it. She had wailed just as Teivel moved to enter her chambers to check on her. She had requested to be alone. What he saw was not human, it was everything he could not describe, an energy of color surrounding her, breaking every near object into pieces. But most of all, the room emanated a red glow.

She was just like *them*.
Only worse.

But he needed proof still. It didn't matter how close of a standing he had to the king, there was nothing he could do that would not land him in a cell without proof or cause to believe that she is a danger to the people. Unfortunately, not everyone shared the Gloh values. Teivel believed that exposing the true danger behind these unnatural people, in a noble way, would finally convince people of the truth. Just because they are less openly present does not mean that they are gone, the midnight market on its own is a large threat. If Dolores made her way to the market after closing, perhaps that could be the proof he needs? He could catch her in the act of purchasing something for ill use and expose her, everyone would see her the way he does. A danger. But the vendors always came with the most stock they could to serve the large crowds, they would not run out for hours.

Nearly every day, Dolores would take a trip to the library to be alone. Harald always said that the time apart for a few hours during the way, away from work and each other, made their relationship better. She would easily spend three to four hours in there. But whenever Teivel, or anyone else for that matter, came to ask her about something or check on her, she was nowhere to be found. Yet she claims she was in the library the entire time. While the towering shelves, filled to the brim with books, might be intimidating at first, once you've spent a few years in the castle, you begin to learn your way around even the most maze-like of places. And unless she was actively moving, just barely evading the people searching for her, there was something else going on. Even more secrets. If only that was enough to convince people, they were all so small-minded and stubborn, too oblivious to see what was right in front of them. But he would not give up, because if he did, his parents died for nothing.

AGE: 15

Kirai and Mischa Malacoda didn't understand why the yearly market was such a hoot each and every year. They had quickly noticed that their neighbors, and everyone else in the village, were all either discussing the preparations they needed to make for their stall or their expectations, and scheduling for the event. It was just a market. They didn't understand. But they didn't voice that, they were far too new to share such opinions without being labeled judgemental. Things in the central village of Gortasia were far different from the small region of Gloh. The only reason they had left their loving, small community was because the Malacoda family had had the honor of being chosen to try and spread the word of their region, the word against the unnaturals plaguing the world around them, plaguing the people. It was a slow thing; they were aware of that. Striking fast and hard had failed them before, and now they knew better. Small steps. The market could be a good way to subtly spread the word, convince people they were most likely not going to see for another year or so, there always seemed to be a struggle to keep the market on the same day.

It was late afternoon by the time the Malacoda spouses left their quaint house in the village to join the craze of the market. Even at this time of day, the crowd still poured in and out of the gaps between the stalls, all struggling to fit into the designated space. Mischa scoffed at the sight from the comfort of their doorframe while Kirai raised an unimpressed brow.

"I don't understand all the excitement," Mischa spoke, her voice was heavy and displayed an accent often labeled as that of a farmer's. With Gloh being such a small community, and such a disliked one, they relied heavily on what they were able to obtain in their home region, mainly being farmed resources and each other.

"Can't be much different than anything you'd find in a shop."

"Yes, darling," Kirai said, his accent the same. "But we can't let their simple excitement stop us from spreading the word of Gloh. Carefully. There is no other way."

"Let's hope they're not too distracted by all the wooden boxes to notice that we're talking to them."

Kirai shot his wife a pained smile, recognizing the truth in her words. The people surrounding them appeared to be *very* easily distracted by a display of *very* mediocre items. And the idea of a midnight market concerned them, it was spoken of in whispers, spread around like a rumor. Nothing good could come of that, but who knew when they reach that point. The market had started as the sun rose, but there was no sign of the crowd thinning out. Especially as they tried to make their way through to find someone to speak with on the matter of *magic*.

They wound up splitting up due to the force of the crowd, each person pushing and squeezing to reach their intended location. Kirai found himself fighting for the attention of an elderly woman picking away at a sugary pastry, while Mischa wished for death as she stood alongside a rather chatty man.

"Did no one teach you manners, boy?" the old woman asked, her white hair a craze in its days-old bun. "You haven't even asked for my name *or* offered yours. I am not interested in conversation with a rude stranger."

"My apologies," Kirai forced out. He hadn't expected the sweet-looking old woman to be so snappy. "My name is Kirai, and you?" He was impatient, and it was showing, but it seemed to be good enough for the old woman.

"Madam Adler will do. What can I help you with then, Kirai?" She took a small bite of the pastry, chewing it slowly. It caught his eye, he was still distracted by the way the old woman spoke and acted that it took him longer than he would admit to his wife for him to register her response.

"I was wondering if you knew anything about this," he lowered his voice and leaned in closer to an unimpressed Madam Adler, "*midnight market.*"

"Of course, I've heard of it," she said. "I was here when the market first began, that one too."

"I've heard that they sell *magical* objects there," he felt incredibly foolish, like a gossiping schoolgirl. But he had to do what must be done, for the good of the people. "Don't you believe that's kind of dangerous? If it fell into the wrong hands…"

Madam Adler sighed, turning over the pastry in her hands. She looked up at him with the expression of a disappointed parent, which at her age she just as well could be. "I am not interested in wasting my time on people who intend to talk poorly of people who don't deserve it," she placed a hand on Kirai's shoulder, "I hope you find a better purpose to life, Kirai. You *and* Mischa." With that, she walked away, taking another bite of her pastry just as Mischa rejoined him. How did she know Mischa's name?

"I could barely get a word in with all his blabbing," Mischa said with a scowl and a sigh. "Maybe it's best if we just go this *midnight market* ourselves and get some sort of proof that it's dangerous. Kirai?" She snapped her fingers in front of his face. "Kirai."

"Sorry." He shook his head out as if to release whatever trance he had been left in. "What were you saying?" Almost the entire interaction he had had with Madam Adler slipped his mind completely, only leaving him with the fact that it had been unsuccessful. That was all he needed to know, really.

"*I was saying* that we should take a look at the midnight market ourselves." Mischa's arms were crossed over her chest, her eyes hard as they stared at her husband. He was rubbing at the light trace of stubble on his chin, pondering the suggestion. It was only when he looked up to meet her eyes that he realized that she was less than happy.

"So," he said, "your interaction didn't go well either?"

Her eyebrows lowered and furrowed. "I'm going back to the house until this shit is over." She gestured at the rows of stalls and people crowding them, turning on her heel and making her way back towards their quaint village house, leaving her husband behind.

Standing so close to the remaining crowd felt like a danger in itself to Kirai, who mere moments after his wife had walked away had to scramble to dodge the barely conscious body of a middle-aged man who seemed to favor the ale stand placed somewhere in the market. The man stumbled about, attempting to clutch whatever was within reach to keep his balance upright, if that was even possible in his current state. But no one seemed to mind, maybe it was something they were used to. The Malacoda's kept their socialization limited for the most part, worried that if they made *too much* of an effort that someone might grow suspicious of their chosen conversation topics. Occasionally, they would need to put up the act of interest in whatever current happenings went on in the lives of their neighbors and work companions. It was all very uninteresting. And not once had they by their own free will visited the local pub, which they had been invited to before, claiming they always went to bed early. It was possible that whoever this fool was, was a regular at the pub or at the very least, the market. That was what he chose to believe, preferring not to face the potential fact that the people he surrounded himself with were truly so captivated by the meager food and trinkets. Blissful ignorance was a way of life.

As the stock ran dry, the crowd began to dwindle and grow thin. While Mischa remained in the house, and Teivel spent time at the castle, Kirai had watched it all from a distance. The last couple of hours had been spent observing, and judging, from the shadows of the village. As the vendors cleaned up their stalls and left, they were soon replaced by a different group, carrying less stock, and each dressed in darker clothing. They brought no lanterns with them, most of them hadn't even brought a light source at all, a candle being the most to be placed down other than the few items for sale. Then, similarly to new vendors, a smaller group of people began to scan the few staffed stalls. The sun had gone down at this point, leaving the village in a blanket of darkness, only broken through by the scarce sources of lights in people's windows and the few candles placed outside.

"There you are," Mischa said from behind him, stepping to stand by his side, watching over the midnight market. The sun may have gone down but it was far from midnight still. "Well, at least it exists."

"Is Teivel home?"

"No, they sent someone down from the castle to inform me that he planned on spending the night. He'll be back sometime tomorrow." She leaned her body up against the wall of the nearest house, eyes trained on the fog-ridden market that had been left behind. "Which one should we go to?"

The couple scanned the manned stalls, looking for something… dangerous. Mischa's eyes landed on a stall near the very edge, it had only a small candle next to darkness in the stalls surrounding it, separating it in a way. From a distance it appeared to be run by a woman with cascading black hair, which upon closer inspection was actually a deep purple, striking against her pale skin. Laid in front of her were six orbs which seemed to have been pressed down into a disc, emanating various shades of pink light.

"Can I interest you in something?" the woman asked. She had dark brown eyes, similar to that of a doe. Her hands were braced to the sides of the stall, awaiting their response.

"What do they do?" Kirai asked, reaching his hand out to touch one of the flattened orbs, the color of blush. The woman's hand shot out, nearly making contact with Kirai, stopping him mid motion. His hand hovered over the flattened orb as his eyes met hers, both of their arms extended.

"No touching," the purple-haired woman said. Kirai pulled his arm back, the woman following suit. "Sorry, wouldn't want anything bad to happen. They're illusion discs, you can tie a memory of a person or thing to see it again."

As per usual, Kirai's mind, and Mischa's too for that matter, immediately found the negative aspects of the product. The dangerous ones that are the reason magic should be outlawed across the world. Surely something of the sort could be used for quite the nefarious reasons, leading to undoable harm. And this woman was a part of it, she was enabling it. The couple exchanged a glance before turning back to the seller.

"That seems… well, it seems like it could be dangerous," Mischa said, crossing her arms over her stomach.

"If you buy it from someone careless."

The seller's eyes were trained on Mischa, who stared right back, neither of them were paying much attention to Kirai.

"And how do we know you're not?" he said, reaching over to one of the other discs, this one a darker pink. The purple-haired woman did not have the time to stop him at his second attempt, instead watching with wide eyes as he picked it up. Nothing happened. Until something did.

He turned to look at his wife, a pit forming in his stomach at the sight of her.

A man was stood in front of her, hands wrapped tightly around her throat. Her eyes were bulging out of her head, mouth open in a silent scream that never made it past her throat. It was pure instinct to reach inside of pocket and pull out the small dagger he kept concealed there, plunging it deep into the back of the attacker. His other hand held onto the disc, resting on the shoulder of the man threatening to kill his wife. Mischa's expression turned from horror, to pain, to anger. But Kirai saw none of this.

What Kirai saw was the man turning to face him, the attacker lacked a face, made of nothing but smooth curves where a nose, a mouth, eyes should have been. There was only olive skin.

But that did not stop him.

He fought back with all he had in him. Even as the attacker brought his leg down, hard, against Kirai's lower leg filling his ears with a sickening crack as his leg was left pointing in an unnatural angle. His hand was still tightly wrapped around the pink disc, using it as an advantage and swinging it down over the attacker's head, staining it with blood. Moving was difficult, but the fight continued, nonetheless. The dagger continued swinging, being driven through a hand, an arm, a shoulder. He was aiming for the neck but the attacker put up a good fight. More sickening cracks were soon to follow as bones were snapped and fractured. The disc began to follow suit, small cracks spreading across its surface. Features appeared and disappeared just as fast on the attacker's smoothed face. What magic was he wielding?

Kirai and the attacker fell to the ground, bleeding and mangled, no longer able to support their bodies. The disc fell out of his hand, weakened, it hit the ground and burst into pieces, a puff of pink smoke escaping it. Kirai turned to look at the attacker once more, pain spreading throughout his entire body from the failed fight. But there was no attacker lying by his side, there was only his wife. Her blood mixed with his, seeping into the ground underneath a tree. She was the last thing he saw, too weak to turn away. The seller with her deep purple hair had busied herself with packing up the remaining discs during their illusioned fight and ran away.

If you ever encounter someone selling illusion discs, do be careful. What the seller with the long purple hair, whose name you will learn to be Brangwen, was trying to tell the hateful couple was that the unbound discs were dangerous to touch with your bare hands. Because when it lacks a specific memory, it will simply conjure an illusion related to something already on your mind. It doesn't need to be a memory. As witnessed with Kirai and Mischa Malacoda, whose time was most often spent thinking of all the ways magic was dangerous and how it could one day kill them, it created the illusion that it did. For future reference.

The following morning there was nothing wrong as the young Teivel Malacoda strolled down the hill towards the village, his sights set on the small house he lived in. He had spent the night in the castle at the courtesy of his friend Harald, the future king of Gortasia. Quite the friend to make.

He wasn't worried about his parents being upset or wondering where he was, one of the servants had been kind enough to inform his parents on their way home. So he strolled contently through the village, taking in the leftovers from yesterdays market, the stalls had all been cleaned, ready to be used by the locals wishing to sell their items. It was still early in the morning, the village was empty, most locals still sleeping off the excitement leftover from the market. His parents were probably still in the house, awake, but wishing to avoiding any one-sided conversations until work the next day.

Teivel stopped short two or three stalls away from the end of the designated market space at the sight of something dark in the grass. He could see the crown of a tree towering above, but he doubted that was the source of whatever had stained the ground in such a way. Slowly, he walked closer, watching the stain grow larger with every step. Until he saw it.

Bodies.

Two of them.

Kirai. Mangled.

Mischa. Mangled.

His parents. Mangled.

He couldn't breathe. The sight of his parents' bodies, limbs broken, pointing. Their eyes were glossed over and still. The blood was dry. They had been there for a while. Tears pooled from his eyes; a scream escaped his throat but no one came. And they were still dead.

Teivel looked around helplessly for some sign of what may have happened to his parents while he was happily spending the night away from them. His eyes scanned the stalls, the tree, the houses, the grass. Next to their bodies lay a broken… something. It looked glasslike, and pink. He leaned down to touch it, stopping just centimeters above. His hand hovered over it, and instantly he knew. Magic. He had been warned to stay far away from it his entire life, that it was something to be eradicated. Magic had killed his parents, or at the very least, someone wielding it.

AGE: 46

The library was as empty as ever, any servants still in the castle working on finishing up their last tasks before they can head home for the day. Cleaning and cooking to make sure everything was well for the royal family before they themselves would be given the opportunity to enjoy the market. Teivel had never told Harald what he had found that day, about the twisted bodies and blood-stained grass. He had returned to the castle in tears, grief and fear had overtaken him on the walk back up to the castle, and he was sobbing by the time he reached the great doors. All he said was that his parents were no longer alive, and right then and there Harald had rushed to find his father to ask if Teivel could stay with them, he had no one else.

Every damn time Teivel went into the library to look for Dolores, he could never find her. And it would be far too lucky if they were simply moving in opposite directions during each visit. It was unrealistic for that to be the truth. Meaning that the only logical solution would be for there to be some form of secret room hidden inside of the library walls. All he had to do was find it.

Easier said than done.

The royal advisor wandered the library for what felt like hours. Weaving between towering shelves, running has hands along spines of books that caught his eye. There was nothing unusual to be found other than a couple of missed cobwebs he would have to inform the servants of. The idea of spiders crawling across the royal family while they were trying to enjoy a good book sent shivers down his spine. But that was irrelevant to the situation at hand. Back to searching.

Teivel muttered a string of curses under his breath. At this speed both Harald and Dolores would have returned to the castle before he had the chance to find anything at all. Or if the universe felt especially cruel, right when he found whatever secrets were hidden here.

He climbed the ladder up to the library's second floor, much to the disdain of his aching joints. They really ought to replace that ladder with a staircase, it's just impractical the way it is. He stalked the floor, scanning the shelves on his side while simultaneously keeping an eye on the ones ahead of him. A short second before turning back to face ahead, there was a red light. He snapped his head back so quickly he worried his neck would break, but it didn't. It still hurt, though. But there was no light when he turned back, maybe he was in need of glasses, or he was going mad. And then, right as he was about to continue down, the light returned. It was pulsating with uneven breaks, seemingly coming from somewhere in between two of the shelves. He grabbed at the shelf to the left of the ominous light, pulling with all his might. He was surprised to find that the shelf moved, but not outwardly as if you were pulling it out, moreso in a curve as if you were opening a door. And as it turned out, that was exactly what he was doing.

He couldn't believe it.

He had actually found it.

Well, obviously he had found it, that was what he set out to do.

This changes everything.

Hidden away behind the bookshelf was an entire office which he could only assume, albeit confidently, belonged to Queen Dolores. There was a sparse shelf tucked into the corner to the left, a desk with a glowing book and unlit lantern on the right, a worn carpet on the floor. The book giving off the light which had revealed the location of the secret office to Teivel held the title of *Learnings of Color Magic.* He had been right all along. But this wasn't proof enough, a book simply *about* magic would not prove that she inhabited it herself, he needed more. Teivel turned to the bookshelf on the other side of the room, looking over the few books placed in it. His hand wrapped around one in red leather, stamped into the cover and inked with gold stood *Property of Dolores Dolion.* And he had struck gold indeed.

He continued to flip through the pages until there was nothing left to turn. *This* was the confirmation he needed. The proof that all of the beliefs he had about Dolores were true. *Reason* to finally get rid of her, in one way or another. Teivel slammed the book shut and placed it back onto the shelf, eyeing it suspiciously. There was already one secret bookshelf door in the library itself, why couldn't there be one within the secret room as well? To test the theory, he gripped the edge of the bookshelf, and pulled. It groaned at the movement but opened, nonetheless. Hidden away behind the bookshelf was a tunnel. How odd. He wondered where it might lead and considering he had already found everything he needed in the secret office, he stepped inside, pulled the bookshelf back against the wall, and walked.

It was like walking through a slim hallway, which he assumed was hidden inside of the castle walls. But why keep two secret entrances? It seemed unlikely that Dolores used them both to access the hidden space, considering how she always shared the fact that she was headed to the library, it would be far easier to simply duck away and travel through the walls. Losing track of someone in the entirety of the castle was much simpler than in the library alone. He wondered where the tunnel would lead.

After several minutes of stumbles and turns, Teivel found himself at what appeared to be a dead end. At first. After further inspection and peeping through the subtle eye holes made in the wall in front of him, he recognized it as the third floor hallway, just around the corner from the king and queen's chambers. He couldn't believe that he had never noticed the holes made into the painting hanging on the wall, but at this moment it helped him confirm that he would not get caught exiting the secret tunnel. It certainly would be a lot more convenient for

Dolores to make use of the tunnel rather than going to the library where her absence was much more noticeable. As proven by Teivel. Carefully, he pushed the painting open, stepped down, and pushed it shut again. He stared up at it, feeling deceived. How long had those holes been there, it made sense why he had never noticed them before, they were well concealed. He looked around the hall to confirm that the was still alone, then looked around the corner to see Dolores walking out of the royal chambers. He ducked behind the wall, peeking out ever so slightly to watch her walk away. His eyes traveled to the door. Harald was probably still inside.

"Harald?" Teivel asked, slowly opening the door. He had knocked but gotten no response. However, he could hear footsteps inside. Had it been anyone else, they never would have dared to enter the royal chambers without express permission, but the two of them had known each other for decades. They were past that now. So he stepped inside to see Harald a mess. His face was red, eyes puffy as he wiped a tear away with sweaty hands. "Harald."

"Teivel...," Harald said, wiping at his face once more. He was turned away from the door, only turning to face his friend and advisor once he believed himself to be presentable. "I didn't hear you come in."

"What is wrong?"

"Dolores doesn't trust me," his eyes glossed over one more as he spoke, his voice cracking at the end. Teivel stepped forward and placed a hand on his shoulder.

"Tell me, friend," he said. "What is troubling you?"

Everything fell into place. He had never needed to find the office hidden away in the library, the book with teachings of color magic, the journals recounting Dolores's training with a local witch. Harald trusts him, that was all he needed. That is all he has ever needed. His parents moved their family to Gortasia in order to spread the word of the dangers of magic, and he had entered the true heart of the kingdom to do just that. He had befriended the king, become his friend, his advisor, his brother. And Harald told him everything. Dolores's red magic, the midnight ware necklace she had been gifted, the conversation with the witch. Their argument was not of importance, but it could prove to be useful, seeds of doubt had already been planted without the help of Teivel. Everything had just become a whole lot easier.

"Have you considered that the reason she has not confirmed your suspicion is because she plans on using them for personal gain?" Teivel proposed, an eyebrow raised.

"What are you saying?" Harald was skeptical, but he could be convinced.

"If she truly belongs to the magic of red, she could prove to be dangerous. To both you and to this kingdom. It would not require much effort for her to take the throne for herself and rule with fear to her name." Harald stood in front of him, poring over his words. Everyone can be convinced, even a king. Especially if they trust you. With a hand on Harald's shoulder he continued, "I suggest we handle the issue before it grows out of hand. I will offer you any service. My lord."

Harald looked up at him pained eyes. "You make a good point. It… it is something that must be stopped," with every word it became more and more clear he was holding back tears, putting a strong front as king, "but I wish to speak with her first."

Wait, what?

"My lord, I am not sure that is *safe*. A single moment alone with you is all she needs to-"

Harald put a hand up in the air, pushing past the advisor. "I am going to speak with my wife." He walked out of the room, leaving Teivel alone. Teivel was alone. In the shared chambers of Harald and *Dolores*.

His eyes made their way over to Dolores side of the room where a cluttered vanity was pushed up against the wall between the common room and her bedroom. A smirk made its way onto his face. He threw a look over his shoulder at the door to check if Harald had changed his mind and returned, but seeing no one there, he walked over to the vanity. He stood hunched over the table, picking at each individual item for something that might help his cause. Just because Harald had agreed to his plans, didn't mean that he would be willing to kill his wife. It would be luck if he found something else hidden away in her own chambers, luck he feared he might need.

"Teivel," a voice behind him sounded. It was a voice he instantly recognized. His back straightened as the door clicked shut. He turned to face her.

"Dolores," he said. He plastered a polite smile on his face, hoping to simply move on as if nothing had happened. His eyes flitted to the blood red gem resting on the table. A midnight ware, given to her by a witch.

"Care to tell me what you are doing here?" she said. "Without Harald here there is hardly any reason for you remain in our quarters. And going through my things."

Is this what happened to his parents all those years ago? Did they find themselves in an unfortunate situation such as this one and the horrid creature who killed them attacked, acted on their anger without hesitation just because they could? He would not let it happen to him. He knew what she was, that gave him power.

"I know what you are, Dolores." Her expression remained strong and unmoving, but he knew this was more than she was expecting. "Yes, I know all about your red magic. You're a danger to this kingdom, to your own family!" Teivel struggled to keep the level of his voice in check, risking it growing to a shout which would surely get the attention of anyone passing by in the hall. Whether that be a measly servant or the king himself.

"Then you know I am prepared to defend myself if you decide that your lies must take a violent turn." A red circle played at the edges of her hazel irises. She was threatening him. He would not accept.

Teivel closed the distance between them in few quick strides. His hands braced against her shoulders, shoving her away and down to the floor. Just as the door opened. Harald was back.

"What is going on here?" He didn't sound angry. More… dumbfounded at the situation he has found before him. He closed the door like you always would, with a gentle click.

Teivel stood slightly hunched over with his arms somewhat extended, still in the position he pushed Dolores over. He looked down at her, the red had inched closer to her pupils but hadn't taken over fully just yet. But that was enough.

"She attacked me," Teivel said, placing both hands on his chest, fabricating a pain in his voice, a pleading. "Harald, I told you she was dangerous, I just… I didn't expect it so soon. You can see it in her eyes."

Hesitantly, Harald followed Teivel's line of sight down to Dolores laying at his feet. She was pushed up on her side, looking up at the two men in disbelief. Indeed, her eyes still displayed remnants of magic never used, but it was convincing. It was exactly what Teivel wanted. She turned her head back to Teivel, the red pulsating and moving, an anger clear on her face. This time, it was more than a threat, it was a promise.

Teivel threw his head in all directions, searching for a defense weapon. First good thing would do. Yes, the fireplace, he looked at the logs stacked in front of it, then at the iron fire poker. Yes, that would do. He scurried to the side of the room and wrapped his hand around the fire poker, it was cold in his hand. He turned back to the rulers with a fire in his eyes, a sinister smile playing on his lips. Dolores was slowly moving, pushing herself up, while Harald was seemingly contemplating life itself as he was forced to face the reality that his wife created a danger to everything he held dear. And as the royal advisor, and the king's closest friend, it was his duty to do whatever it took to protect him. So with the fire poker held tightly in both of his hands, the stepped forward and drove it deep down into Dolores's side before she had the opportunity to stand, nevertheless strike. He was out of breath when he let go, his heart was beating quickly but he was not scared. The smile on his face continued to grow as he watched the pain on her face as she reached to take hold of the fire poker, a small amount of blood had formed around it, staining her light blue dress the same as the red stained her hazel eyes.

She wrapped her hand around and pulled out of her flesh with a pained grunt, Harald moved also, kneeling down to meet her. There seemed to not be much thought regarding her next move, acting on instinct more than anything else. Harald was reaching towards her open wound, now spilling blood faster than before, staining the dress further before it hit the floor. He was kneeled beside her when she struck. Driving the fire poker deep into his leg until it made its way out the other side. He yelped and groaned, bracing himself on the floor, he threw his head back in pain when she pulled it back out and threw it aside. She looked at him with regret, eyes glossed over as the reality of what she had just done settled. The king touched at the gnarly wound on his leg, touching the exposed flesh pouring out blood, leaving his fingers slick with it. But still, he kneeled down next to his wife, all of his focus lasered in on her. One hand on top of the other, he rested it on her wound and pressed, more blood staining his hands. It seeped through the cracks in his fingers, he stared down at it in horror. His eyes widened ever so slightly, his expression was stone but you could tell. He pulled back his hands, staring down at the open palms painted red. He was far away but still there in the room where it all happened. He struggled to stand on his wounded leg but managed, leaning up against the wall for support as he continued to stare. The blood on his hands was the only thing to exist, the room had faded. What happens now?

Teivel turned back to the fireplace, the fire poker was too far away but he couldn't let her get away with it. Harald was distracted enough that he wouldn't be a problem. He had to act fast. His eyes stuck on the pile of logs, never letting go as he leaned down and gripped one in his hand. Dolores was still turned to look back at Harald while putting pressure on her wound with one hand. It wasn't doing much, she had lost a lot of blood already, evident by the amount that surrounded her. It was all over the floor; it was all over her dress. You might not even realize it was originally a light blue. He stalked over and pushed at her shoulder with his foot, it didn't make much strength to knock her down on her back, she was weak now.

He planted his feet on her either side of her waist. His smile was wide on his face, reaching from one ear to the other, his breathing was heavy, he was happy. What he felt was indescribable, it was a sort of happiness, power, that he had not felt in decades, if ever. He might never find the person that killed his parents, but he can still take revenge on those he can find. Starting with Dolores.

He swung down with the log held in both hands, hitting her square in the face. Her nose bloodied, forced to be at an unnatural angle. She opened her mouth to speak.

He hit her again.

A spot of blood formed between her eyebrows, trailing down her continuously bleeding nose.

He hit her again.

The white of her eyes turned red, seeping until there was nothing left to cover.

He hit her again.

She didn't try to fight back.

He hit her again.

She had stopped moving.

He hit her again.

The blood had splattered on his face, on the edge of the log. It was warm, sticky. It felt comforting to him. He stared down at her lifeless body, the indent and mess of exposed flesh created in her face. Her lips were parted. He liked to think that it was to release a scream, or plead, that never made it out.

King Harald dropped back down to the floor, to his knees. Teivel thought perhaps it was because of the pain in his leg, but he looked over to see him looking up from the palms of his hands and to his wife. Bloodied and beat.

"You have to move!" Teivel said, he made his voice out to sound desperate, he needed to be convincing even if the king was barely able. "I dare not speak of what may happen if you are caught. We must move quickly."

He reached over to Harald's shoulder, he stood, wincing at the pain shooting up from his leg. "Your highness?"

Harald blinked, bracing himself on the wall, leaving a bloody handprint on the wallpaper. "What?"

"You should go and get washed up, if anyone sees you, and *this.*" he gestured down at the body at their feet, "things would not end well for you."

He nodded, struggling to tear his eyes away from the body even as his hand found the door handle, even as he pushed it down and took a step outside. Once Harald had stepped out into the hall in search for a washroom, Teivel clicked the door shut, bracing both hands against it. He looked back at the body on the floor, he needed to get this cleaned up, and fast.

He wiped his face with his sleeve several times over to get rid of the blood staining him. He stepped out into the hall himself, looking both ways before walking down as if nothing was wrong. And nothing was, but there was still a problem in need of fixing. And the general would sure to keep it a secret. If only he could find the drunk bastard. It was still early enough in the day for him to still be on the clock, and he better be. He already owed

Teivel enough favors for all of the other times he had had to cover for him when skipped work to spend time at the pub, or the times he showed up drunk to work after spending time at the pub. That man was ridiculous but trustworthy enough to keep his mouth shut about a situation like this.

"Tristan!" Teivel called out once he reached the guard's quarters in one of the lower levels of the castle. He noticed the general dozing off on a chair in the corner of the room, an empty mug of wine lay by one of chair's legs. He walked up and kicked the chair out, causing it to tip over against the wall, and effectively waking the drowsy general. "Wake up, you bastard. I need you to do something for me."

"Don't you always?" Tristan said in a yawn. He pushed the chair back into its correct position and leaned back on it, looking up at Teivel.

"Unless you want me to report some wine being taken from the royal wine cellar," Teivel picked up the mug and gave it a sniff, "oh, and this is a nice one too. I think you'll be glad to help me. Honored even."

"What do you need this time?"

"I need your help taking care of a body."

"Who'd you kill this time? The queen?" Tristan chuckled, combined with a light slap on his knee. He looked up at Teivel to see that his expression had remained still, serious. "You- did you-"

"I need the body moved to the graveyard, she can be placed in the mausoleum, ask any servants you trust to clean up and inform the child, the king is still processing." Teivel stood with his back straight, looking down at Tristan who was still shocked. "I want this done as soon as possible, so move."

"Right, yes."

The general stood up from the chair and awkwardly stumbled out of the room, leaving Teivel to wonder just how much wine he had swiped. But he trusted that General Tristan would perform the duties asked of him well, the body would be moved and cleaned, and young Anwir would be informed. There was not much left to do now. Harald could handle himself alone, he needed the time to process what had happened, in whatever way he chose. But the people must be informed as well, and the only appropriate person to deliver such news would be

Harald. Unfortunately, he was in no state to prepare such a thing, he would need to write a speech. Fortunately, Teivel would be happy to lift that burden off of his already heavy shoulders.

People of Gortasia, I come to you today as your king.

Unfortunately, I bear heavy news, news that have devastated my family, and perhaps you too. A great sorrow has been brought upon us with the passing of your beloved queen, Dolores. It is uncertain what led to this, but we believe it to be a horrible accident that has taken her from us all. We will move forward and make our best attempts to adapt during this trying time. I expect from all you your respect as my son and I, Prince Anwir, keep away from the public eye, and enter of a period of solitude to properly grieve this loss. Your time and your person here is appreciated, you are all loved. Queen Dolores will continue to watch over you from the heavens, and she will not be forgotten.

Thank you.

Acknowledgements

First off, I want to apologize to my mom for handing her another dark and murderous story that may or may not cause her concern for what is going on inside of my mind. Thank you for reading it anyway, I promise it won't always be this bad.

And thank you to Zero, for, as always, putting up with me and taking the time to read what I write (even though at the time of writing this your evil internet has not allowed you to do so), but I look forward for you to read my future work and to hear your reactions to what is going to happen with the hopes of finally getting a picture of you crying because of it.